THE USBORNE
FIRST BOOK OF
AMERICA

Louisa Somerville

Illustrated by Roger Fereday
Designed by Mary Cartwright

Contents

With thanks to
Bill Carter, Barry Kernfeld, Sally McMurry, Anne Millard, Elizabeth Murphy, Joan Phaup,
Charlotte Priest, Louise Reynolds, Katie Richards, Tammy Riser Jones, Mark Simmonds,
Wendy Stanley, Carey Starn, Mary Turner, Holly Weiss.
With thanks also to all those at the Focus information center for expatriates, who checked
the information in this book.

About America

The United States of America is a huge country. Some parts are crowded with people, while other areas are deserted. It is one of the world's richest and most powerful nations; yet some people are very poor.

Fifty states make up the country. On this map, the states are grouped into regions, shown in different colors. There are detailed maps of each region later in the book.

In this book, some names have been shortened.

The words "National" and "State" are left out of place names. For example, Zion Natonal Park is just called Zion Park.

The United States of America is called "the United States" for short, or the letters USA are used.

The word "Indians" is used for American Indians because they are usually known by that name.

North and South America

This is a map of the continents of North and South America. The United States, Canada and Mexico are the main countries of North America.

▲ Hawaii is an American state. It is a group of islands in the Pacific Ocean, far away from the mainland. Beautiful beaches and hot weather make it popular for vacations.

Facts about the United States

The USA is the fourth largest country in the world. It is more than 3,000m between the East and West coasts.

▲ Alaska is much further north than the other states. Canada lies between Alaska and the rest of the USA.

The major cities are New York City, Los Angeles, Chicago, Houston and Philadelphia.

Washington D.C. is the capital city.

Almost 250 million people of many races live in the USA.

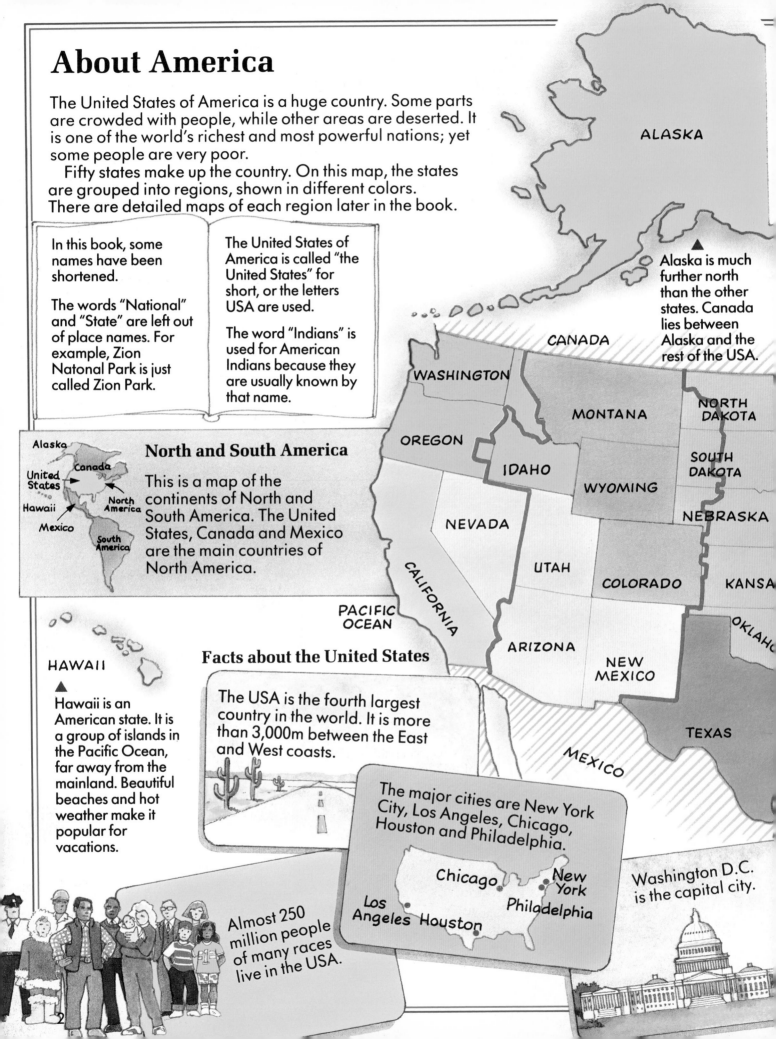

Time zones

The USA is so big that parts of it are in different time zones. The clocks go back one hour for each zone you cross going west. So when it is 9 a.m. in New York, it is only 6 a.m. in Los Angeles.

West

East

New York

Los Angeles

The Stars and Stripes

The United States flag is nicknamed the Stars and Stripes. There are 13 stripes. They stand for the 13 states that first formed the United States long ago. There are also 50 stars, one for each state there is now.

The border between the USA and Canada runs through the middle of these lakes.

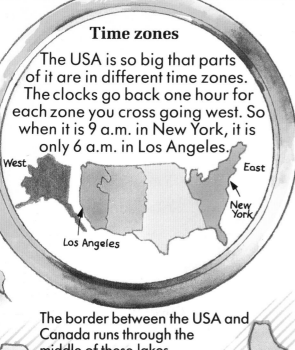

MAINE
VT
NH
NEW YORK
MA
CT
MICHIGAN
WISCONSIN
PENNSYLVANIA
OHIO
INDIANA
ILLINOIS
WEST VIRGINIA
RI
NJ
DE
MD
KENTUCKY
VIRGINIA
TENNESSEE
NORTH CAROLINA
SOUTH CAROLINA
MISSISSIPPI
ALABAMA
GEORGIA
FLORIDA
ATLANTIC OCEAN
GULF OF MEXICO

Each gray line on the map stands for a time zone.

On the map, the names of some states have been shortened. Here are their full names.

CT   Connecticut
DE   Delaware
MA   Massachusetts
MD   Maryland
NH   New Hampshire
NJ   New Jersey
RI   Rhode Island
VT   Vermont

The USA produces more beef, corn, milk and many other foods than any other country.

The longest river is the Mississippi. It flows for over 2,370m.

The highest mountain is Mount McKinley in Alaska. It is 20,320ft high.

The USA is a republic with an elected President. Americans vote for a new President every four years.

Each of the 50 states has a state capital where its government meets. On the maps in this book, every capital is shown by a blue star.

The Federal Government governs the whole country. It makes laws about things that affect everyone, such as money and defense.

3

THE·STORY·OF·AMERICA

In prehistoric times, hunters crossed from Siberia to Alaska. Gradually, they settled all over North and South America. Each tribe developed its own language, clothes and food.

In 1492, Christopher Columbus sailed from Spain. He landed on an island off America, in what we call the West Indies. He thought he had reached India. He called the people who lived there "Indians".

Many more explorers came from Europe. The Spanish conquered parts of the south. The French explored the far north.

In 1620, the Puritans, a religious group from England, sailed to America. They landed at Plymouth Bay in what is now called New England. They settled in the area. Many died from cold and hunger during the first winter.

The Indians showed the settlers how to fish and plant crops. After the first harvest, they held a feast to thank God. Thanksgiving Day is still celebrated each November.

Some settlers traded with the Indians, but many saw them as enemies. Lots of the Indians were killed or died of diseases brought by settlers.

Many English people set up colonies on the east coast. They were still under British rule and paid taxes to Britain. They hated paying them. They wanted America to be free from British rule. In 1775, the War of Independence began.

George Washington

In 1783, the British lost the war. Thirteen colonies gained independence. They formed the United States of America. In 1789, George Washington was chosen as first President.

More states joined the Union. In 1803, President Thomas Jefferson bought the land between the Mississippi River and the Rocky Mountains from France. It doubled the size of the nation.

Pioneers (settlers) moved west in search of farmland. Often they took the Indians' lands. Some went by river. Others followed trails made by fur traders. They traveled in groups of covered wagons, known as wagon trains.

In 1869, two companies raced from the east and west coasts to build the first railway across the country. They joined the rails where they met with a golden spike.

The railway brought more settlers and also the army. They rounded up the Indians and forced them to live in areas called reservations.

Pan for sifting gold.

Gold and silver ore were found in the west. Mining towns sprang up. People moved away when the ore ran out. They left behind "ghost" towns.

The Southern states used slaves to work on their large farms. In the north, there were small farms and factories. They did not need slaves. They wanted to get rid of slavery.

In 1861, the Southern states left the Union of the United States. They formed their own union, called the Confederacy. Civil war broke out. In 1865, the Union won.

During the late 19th and early 20th centuries, many more settlers came from Europe. Some came to escape war and poverty. Others wanted religious and political freedom.

During the 20th century, the USA has fought in major wars, such as the two World Wars and the Korean and Vietnam Wars.

John F. Kennedy

In the early 1960s John F. Kennedy was President. He was shot to death in Dallas, Texas in 1963. During the 1960s, black people demanded their civil rights – equality with whites.

In 1969, astronaut Neil Armstrong was the first person to walk on the moon.

Looking to the future

The USA is a powerful nation. Since 1945, it has been a rival of the USSR, the other "superpower". During the 1990s, the two nations may seek new ways to make peace.

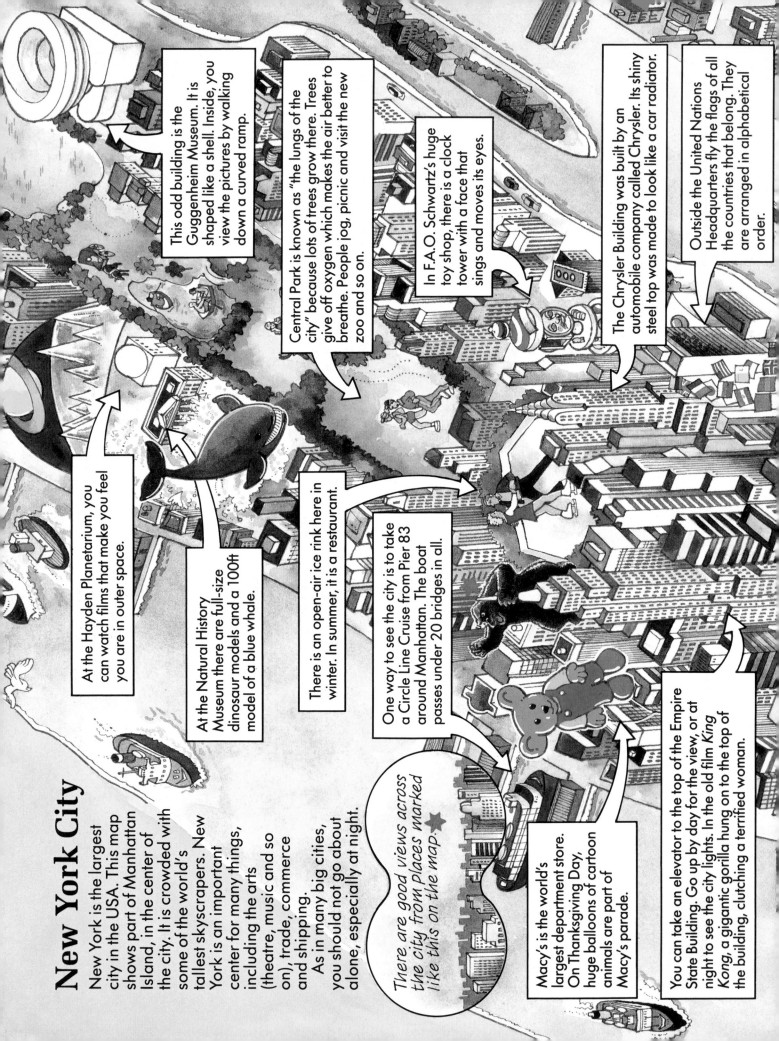

New York City

New York is the largest city in the USA. This map shows part of Manhattan Island, in the center of the city. It is crowded with some of the world's tallest skyscrapers. New York is an important center for many things, including the arts (theatre, music and so on), trade, commerce and shipping.

As in many big cities, you should not go about alone, especially at night.

This odd building is the Guggenheim Museum. It is shaped like a shell. Inside, you view the pictures by walking down a curved ramp.

Central Park is known as "the lungs of the city" because lots of trees grow there. Trees give off oxygen which makes the air better to breathe. People jog, picnic and visit the new zoo and so on.

In F.A.O. Schwartz's huge toy shop, there is a clock tower with a face that sings and moves its eyes.

The Chrysler Building was built by an automobile company called Chrysler. Its shiny steel top was made to look like a car radiator.

Outside the United Nations Headquarters fly the flags of all the countries that belong. They are arranged in alphabetical order.

At the Hayden Planetarium, you can watch films that make you feel you are in outer space.

At the Natural History Museum there are full-size dinosaur models and a 100ft model of a blue whale.

There is an open-air ice rink here in winter. In summer, it is a restaurant.

One way to see the city is to take a Circle Line Cruise from Pier 83 around Manhattan. The boat passes under 20 bridges in all.

There are good views across the city from places marked like this on the map. ★

Macy's is the world's largest department store. On Thanksgiving Day, huge balloons of cartoon animals are part of Macy's parade.

You can take an elevator to the top of the Empire State Building. Go up by day for the view, or at night to see the city lights. In the old film *King Kong*, a gigantic gorilla hung on to the top of the building, clutching a terrified woman.

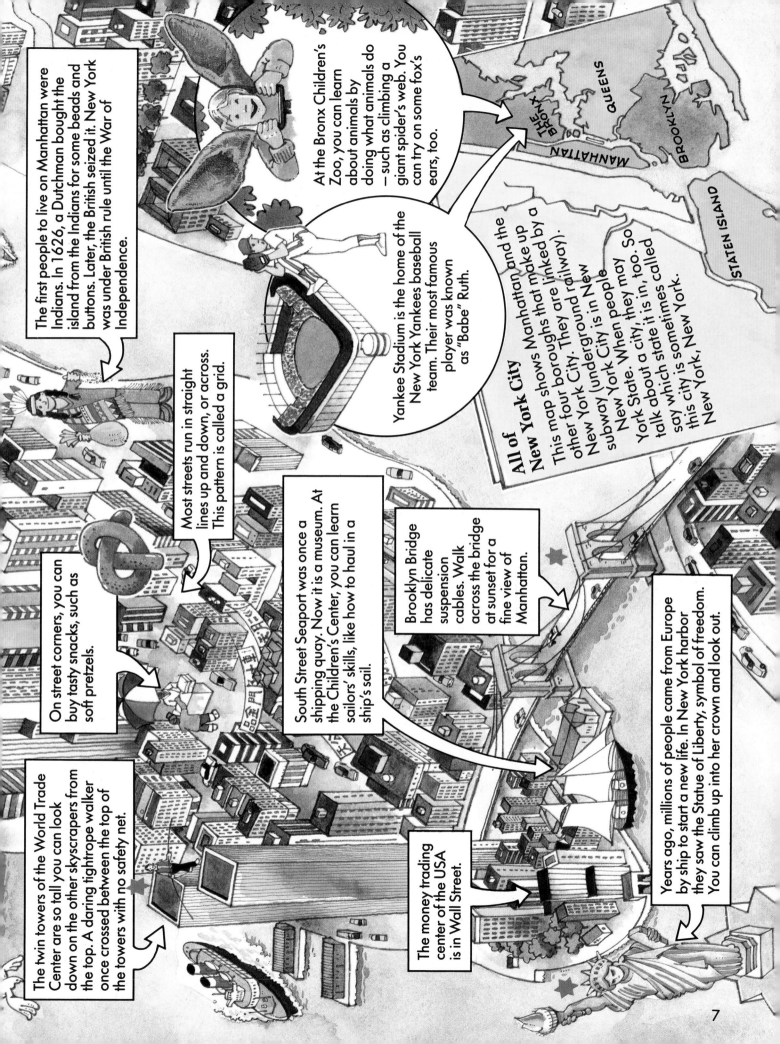

The first people to live on Manhattan were Indians. In 1626, a Dutchman bought the island from the Indians for some beads and buttons. Later, the British seized it. New York was under British rule until the War of Independence.

At the Bronx Children's Zoo, you can learn about animals by doing what animals do – such as climbing a giant spider's web. You can try on some fox's ears, too.

Yankee Stadium is the home of the New York Yankees baseball team. Their most famous player was known as "Babe" Ruth.

Most streets run in straight lines up and down, or across. This pattern is called a grid.

All of New York City
This map shows Manhattan and the other four boroughs that make up New York City. They are linked by a subway (underground railway). New York City is in New York State. When people talk about a city, they may say which state it is in, too. So this city is sometimes called New York, New York.

On street corners, you can buy tasty snacks, such as soft pretzels.

South Street Seaport was once a shipping quay. Now it is a museum. At the Children's Center, you can learn sailors' skills, like how to haul in a ship's sail.

Brooklyn Bridge has delicate suspension cables. Walk across the bridge at sunset for a fine view of Manhattan.

The twin towers of the World Trade Center are so tall you can look down on the other skyscrapers from the top. A daring tightrope walker once crossed between the top of the towers with no safety net.

The money trading center of the USA is in Wall Street.

Years ago, millions of people came from Europe by ship to start a new life. In New York harbor they saw the Statue of Liberty, symbol of freedom. You can climb up into her crown and look out.

THE BRONX

QUEENS

MANHATTAN

BROOKLYN

STATEN ISLAND

7

New England

Most of New England is covered in woodland. There are many pretty villages where white, wooden houses and a church are built around a village green. Today some villages are museums. All along the coast, there are lots of busy fishing ports.

Fall

In the fall (autumn), leaves turn spectacular shades of red, yellow and gold. The maple trees' leaves are especially colorful. Many people come to "leaf-peek". Daily radio reports tell you where to go to see the best leaf colors.

Baked beans

Long ago in winter, people would leave baked beans outside in a cloth-lined pot to freeze. The frozen beans were taken on journeys and chunks were broken off to eat.

Northern Maine is wild, unspoiled country. There is lots of wildlife here, including black bears and moose.

The top of Cadillac Mountain in Acadia Park is where sunlight first touches the United States each morning.

Lobsters are caught off the coast of Maine. Colored buoys mark where lobstermen have laid their traps.

If you visit the White Mountains, you may pass this rock shaped like a face. It is called The Old Man of the Mountains.

Mount Washington is cold and windy. In 1934, the strongest winds ever recorded swept across the mountain, reaching almost 225m per hour. You can get to the top by a cog railway which is over 100 years old.

There are lighthouses all along this rugged coast. Portland Head Light is the oldest.

Vermont is famous for its maple syrup. You can find out how syrup is made at Maple Grove Museum.

Some wooden bridges are covered to protect them from the weather. The longest covered bridge in the country spans the Connecticut River at Windsor. It is 337ft long.

MAINE

★ Augusta

NEW HAMPSHIRE

★ Montpelier

VERMONT

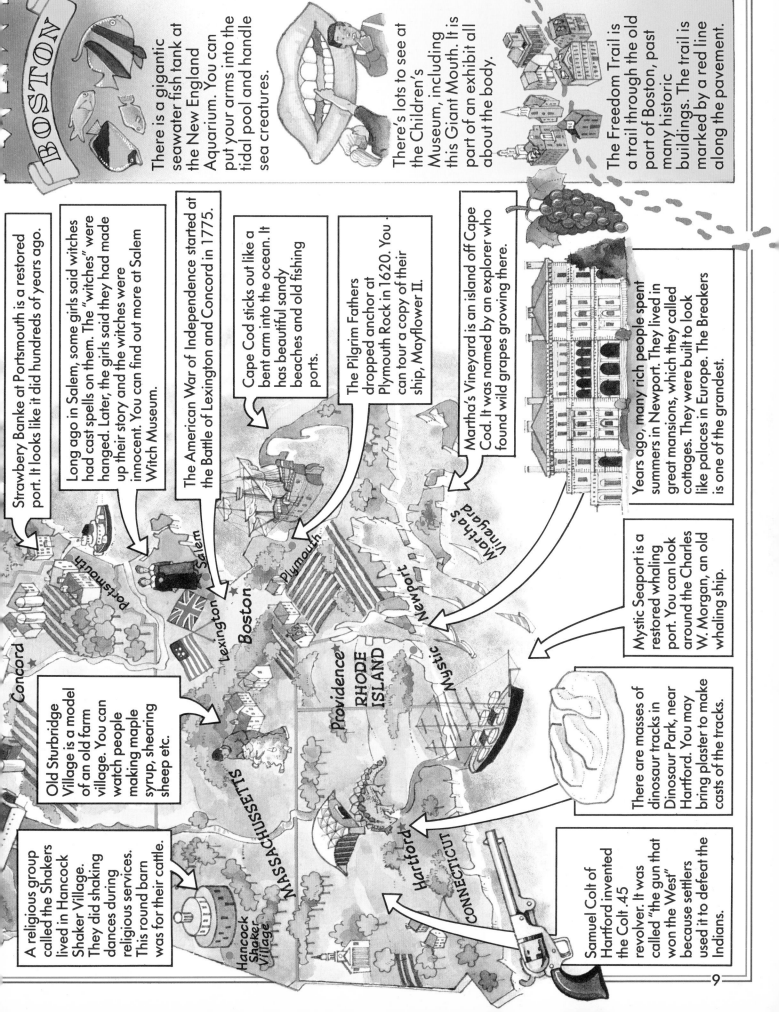

BOSTON

There is a gigantic seawater fish tank at the New England Aquarium. You can put your arms into the tidal pool and handle sea creatures.

There's lots to see at the Children's Museum, including this Giant Mouth. It is part of an exhibit all about the body.

The Freedom Trail is a trail through the old part of Boston, past many historic buildings. The trail is marked by a red line along the pavement.

Strawbery Banke at Portsmouth is a restored port. It looks like it did hundreds of years ago.

Long ago in Salem, some girls said witches had cast spells on them. The "witches" were hanged. Later, the girls said they had made up their story and the witches were innocent. You can find out more at Salem Witch Museum.

The American War of Independence started at the Battle of Lexington and Concord in 1775.

Cape Cod sticks out like a bent arm into the ocean. It has beautiful sandy beaches and old fishing ports.

The Pilgrim Fathers dropped anchor at Plymouth Rock in 1620. You can tour a copy of their ship, Mayflower II.

Martha's Vineyard is an island off Cape Cod. It was named by an explorer who found wild grapes growing there.

Years ago, many rich people spent summers in Newport. They lived in great mansions, which they called cottages. They were built to look like palaces in Europe. The Breakers is one of the grandest.

Mystic Seaport is a restored whaling port. You can look around the Charles W. Morgan, an old whaling ship.

A religious group called the Shakers lived in Hancock Shaker Village. They did shaking dances during religious services. This round barn was for their cattle.

Old Sturbridge Village is a model of an old farm village. You can watch people making maple syrup, shearing sheep etc.

There are masses of dinosaur tracks in Dinosaur Park, near Hartford. You may bring plaster to make casts of the tracks.

Samuel Colt of Hartford invented the Colt .45 revolver. It was called "the gun that won the West" because settlers used it to defeat the Indians.

Concord

Portsmouth

Salem

Lexington

Boston

Plymouth

Martha's Vineyard

Newport

Mystic

Providence

RHODE ISLAND

MASSACHUSSETTS

Hancock Shaker Village

Hartford

CONNECTICUT

9

The Mid-Atlantic states

The United States was "born" in this area. A Declaration of Independence was signed in Philadelphia on July 4, 1776. It said that Americans should be free from Britain. Today a very large number of people live in the Mid-Atlantic states.

Washington D.C. is the capital city of the USA. It is named after George Washington, the first American President. D.C. stands for District of Columbia, another name for the city.

The White House is the President's home. Every President has lived there except George Washington. The house was finished a year after he died.

You can see how handwriting and fingerprints are studied by the police at the FBI (Federal Bureau of Investigation). They investigate serious crimes here.

Famous planes hang from the ceiling at the Air and Space Museum. You can explore inside rockets and watch films about space travel that make you feel as though you are taking part.

Vietnam Veterans Memorial

Washington Monument

The Lincoln Memorial is in memory of President Abraham Lincoln. His speeches are carved on the walls facing his statue.

The Jefferson Memorial is in memory of President Thomas Jefferson. He wrote the Declaration of Independence.

Part of the government, called Congress, meets in the Capitol building. On top of the Capitol is a huge iron dome. No building in the city may be taller than the dome.

Since the Civil War, soldiers have been buried in Arlington Cemetery outside Washington D.C. The graves of many famous people are here, including President John F. Kennedy.

The Kentucky Derby horse races are held in Louisville in May. The Run for the Roses is a famous race.

Daniel Boone was a hunter and trapper. He led the first pioneers that crossed the Appalachian Mountains, through a passage called Cumberland Gap.

Louisville

Frankfort

KENTUCKY

A type of grass called bluegrass grows in Kentucky. It is especially good for horses. It makes the pasture look blue-colored.

The world's longest cave system is at Mammoth Cave.

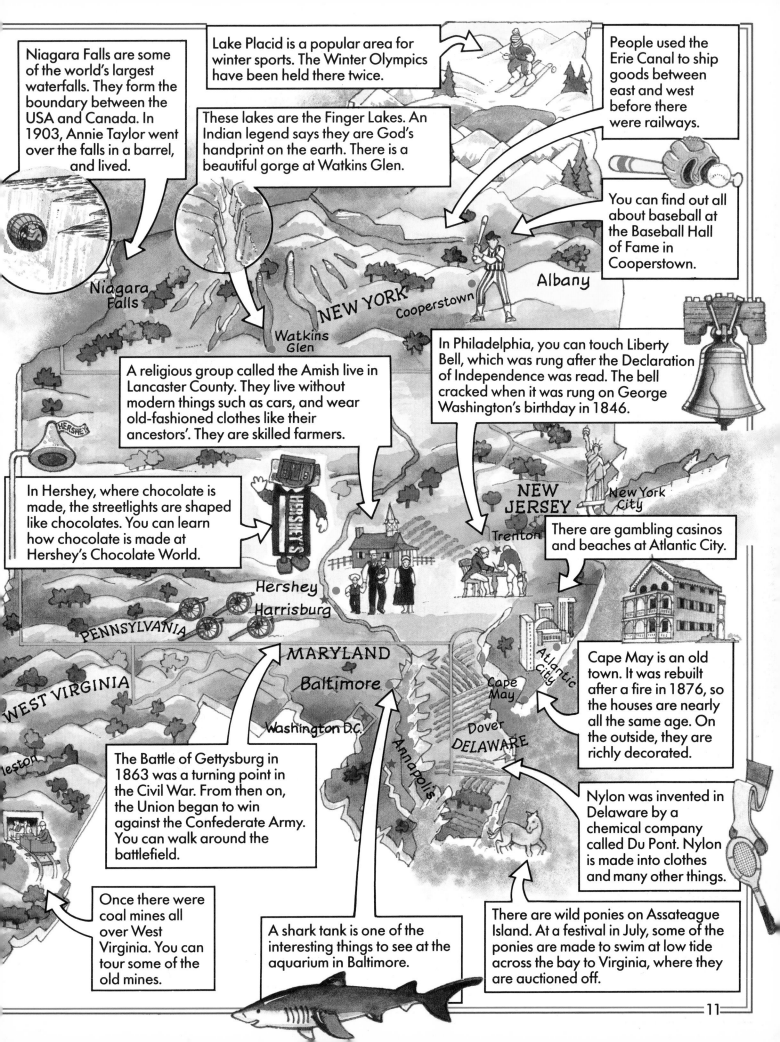

Niagara Falls are some of the world's largest waterfalls. They form the boundary between the USA and Canada. In 1903, Annie Taylor went over the falls in a barrel, and lived.

Lake Placid is a popular area for winter sports. The Winter Olympics have been held there twice.

These lakes are the Finger Lakes. An Indian legend says they are God's handprint on the earth. There is a beautiful gorge at Watkins Glen.

People used the Erie Canal to ship goods between east and west before there were railways.

You can find out all about baseball at the Baseball Hall of Fame in Cooperstown.

In Philadelphia, you can touch Liberty Bell, which was rung after the Declaration of Independence was read. The bell cracked when it was rung on George Washington's birthday in 1846.

A religious group called the Amish live in Lancaster County. They live without modern things such as cars, and wear old-fashioned clothes like their ancestors'. They are skilled farmers.

In Hershey, where chocolate is made, the streetlights are shaped like chocolates. You can learn how chocolate is made at Hershey's Chocolate World.

There are gambling casinos and beaches at Atlantic City.

Cape May is an old town. It was rebuilt after a fire in 1876, so the houses are nearly all the same age. On the outside, they are richly decorated.

The Battle of Gettysburg in 1863 was a turning point in the Civil War. From then on, the Union began to win against the Confederate Army. You can walk around the battlefield.

Nylon was invented in Delaware by a chemical company called Du Pont. Nylon is made into clothes and many other things.

Once there were coal mines all over West Virginia. You can tour some of the old mines.

A shark tank is one of the interesting things to see at the aquarium in Baltimore.

There are wild ponies on Assateague Island. At a festival in July, some of the ponies are made to swim at low tide across the bay to Virginia, where they are auctioned off.

Niagara Falls

NEW YORK

Cooperstown

Albany

Watkins Glen

NEW JERSEY

New York City

Trenton

Hershey

Harrisburg

PENNSYLVANIA

Atlantic City

MARYLAND

Baltimore

Cape May

Dover

DELAWARE

WEST VIRGINIA

Washington D.C.

Annapolis

...leston

Some Southern states

This was one of the first areas to be settled by Europeans. They lived here for many years because the Appalachian Mountains formed a natural barrier to the west. There are many historic old towns and also Civil War sites to explore.

Blackbeard

Blackbeard was a very tall pirate with a long beard. He and his crew plundered ships along the coast of North Carolina. In the end, his ship was chased by the navy. There was a fierce battle near Ocracoke Island and he was killed.

Pocahontas

Pocahontas was an Indian girl. She saved the life of John Smith, an English trader who was about to be killed by Indians at Jamestown. Later she married another Englishman and returned to England with him.

George Washington, the first American President, lived and farmed at Mount Vernon. He owned an immense area of land.

President Thomas Jefferson was an architect. He designed his own house, called Monticello. Inside, there are lots of gadgets designed by him, too, including this writing machine. It made an instant copy as he wrote.

Williamsburg has been restored to look like it did more than 200 years ago. Cobblers, wigmakers and others go about their work in 18th century costume. There are parades with drummers and pipers.

At Jamestown Settlement you can board copies of the ships that brought the first successful settlers from England in 1607.

VIRGINIA

Charlottesville •

Richmond

Jamestown

Williamsburg

The Civil War

There were arguments between the states in the North and South. In 1861, several Southern states left the Union of States and set up their own union, which they called a Confederacy. Civil war broke out.

The fighting began on April 12, 1861 when Confederate troops captured Fort Sumter from Union soldiers. The fort is on an island in Charleston Harbor.

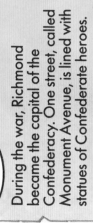

During the war, Richmond became the capital of the Confederacy. One street, called Monument Avenue, is lined with statues of Confederate heroes.

The Civil War ended when General Robert E. Lee, leader of the Confederate army, surrendered at Appomattox in 1865.

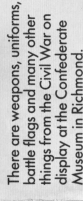

There are weapons, uniforms, battle flags and many other things from the Civil War on display at the Confederate Museum in Richmond.

These flags mark Charleston Harbor, Richmond and Appomattox on the map.

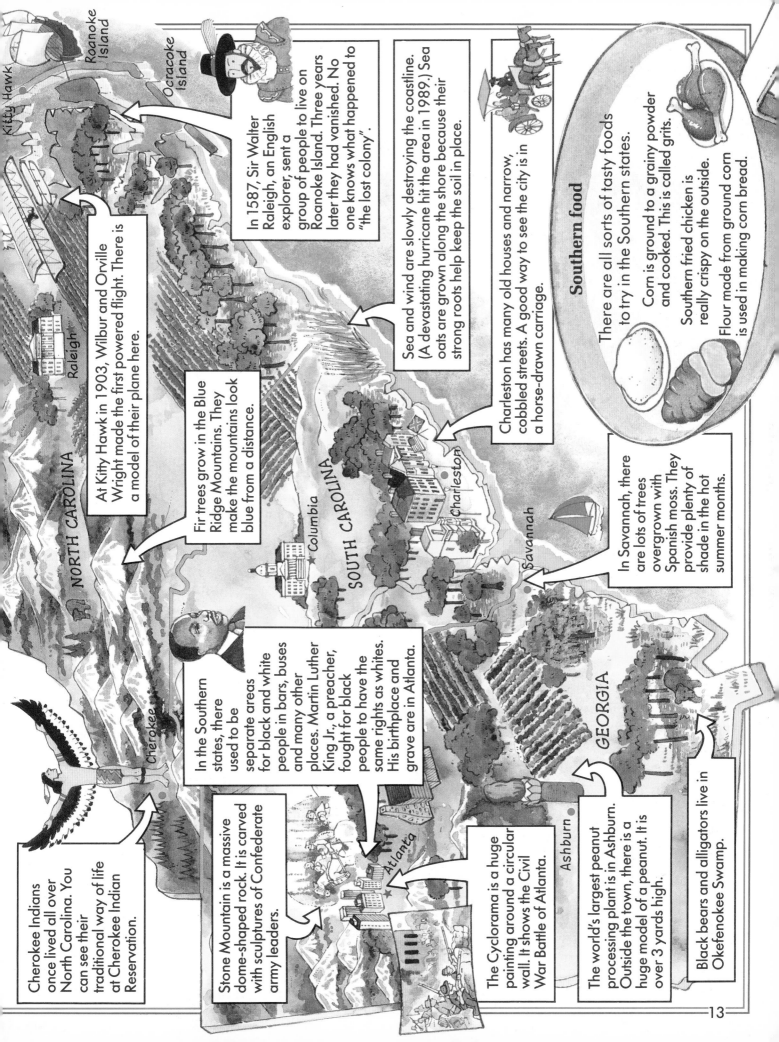

Kitty Hawk

Roanoke Island

Ocracoke Island

Raleigh

NORTH CAROLINA

Cherokee

Columbia

SOUTH CAROLINA

Charleston

Savannah

GEORGIA

Atlanta

Ashburn

At Kitty Hawk in 1903, Wilbur and Orville Wright made the first powered flight. There is a model of their plane here.

In 1587, Sir Walter Raleigh, an English explorer, sent a group of people to live on Roanoke Island. Three years later they had vanished. No one knows what happened to "the lost colony".

Sea and wind are slowly destroying the coastline. (A devastating hurricane hit the area in 1989.) Sea oats are grown along the shore because their strong roots help keep the soil in place.

Charleston has many old houses and narrow, cobbled streets. A good way to see the city is in a horse-drawn carriage.

Fir trees grow in the Blue Ridge Mountains. They make the mountains look blue from a distance.

Southern food

There are all sorts of tasty foods to try in the Southern states.

Corn is ground to a grainy powder and cooked. This is called grits.

Southern fried chicken is really crispy on the outside.

Flour made from ground corn is used in making corn bread.

In Savannah, there are lots of trees overgrown with Spanish moss. They provide plenty of shade in the hot summer months.

Cherokee Indians once lived all over North Carolina. You can see their traditional way of life at Cherokee Indian Reservation.

In the Southern states, there used to be separate areas for black and white people in bars, buses and many other places. Martin Luther King Jr., a preacher, fought for black people to have the same rights as whites. His birthplace and grave are in Atlanta.

Stone Mountain is a massive dome-shaped rock. It is carved with sculptures of Confederate army leaders.

The Cyclorama is a huge painting around a circular wall. It shows the Civil War Battle of Atlanta.

The world's largest peanut processing plant is in Ashburn. Outside the town, there is a huge model of a peanut. It is over 3 yards high.

Black bears and alligators live in Okefenokee Swamp.

Florida

Florida is known as the Sunshine State. People who enjoy hot weather come here at all times of the year. Sometimes there are hurricanes. They are so powerful they can tear down trees and houses.

Pensacola

Tallahassee ★

At different times, Pensacola was ruled by Spain, England, France, the Confederacy and the United States. It is nicknamed the City of Five Flags.

The Blue Angels, a special flying team, give daredevil displays at the Naval Air Station.

Baseball teams come to Florida from all over the United States to train in the Spring.

THEME PARKS

There are lots of theme parks throughout Florida. All of the ones below (except Busch Gardens) are near Orlando.

You can see animals in an African jungle setting at Busch Gardens in Tampa. ▶

At Wet 'n Wild, there is a pool with artificial waves where surfers practice.

Baseball fans can practice their skills at Boardwalk and Baseball.

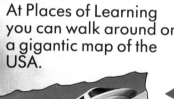

At Places of Learning you can walk around on a gigantic map of the USA.

© The Walt Disney Company

◀ This Monorail takes people around Walt Disney World. It is the world's largest theme park and resort. One area, called EPCOT Center, has a futuristic theme. It is marked by a huge geosphere.

Film studios

Some film companies have studios where you can watch films and shows being made. You can also learn about special effects, etc.

Tarpon Springs is a fishing village where lots of Greek people live. Many types of sponge are sold here. Greek fishermen dive for them in the ocean.

This fisherman is catching stone crabs. He breaks off the large claw for eating. Then he throws the crab back in the water and it grows another claw.

People come to Sanibel Island's beaches to collect shells. There are over 400 types.

The islands on the page opposite are called the Florida Keys. Many ships were wrecked on the coral reef nearby. Glass bottom boats take people out to the reef to see colorful coral and tropical fish.

St. Augustine is the oldest city in the United States. Many of the houses are built of coquina, a limestone made of shells and coral.

There is car racing at Daytona. People drive on the hard, sandy beach, too.

Cypress Gardens is a beautiful park. This revolving platform lifts you high in the air for a good view.

The first explorer

Ponce de León, a Spanish explorer, discovered Florida at Easter in 1513. He was looking for a "fountain of youth" he had heard tales of. He called the land Pascua Florida which means Easter blossoms in Spanish.

There are millions of orange trees in this part of Florida.

Thomas Edison invented the lightbulb. He wanted to put up electric lights in Fort Myers, where he lived. He was not allowed to because people feared it would keep their cows awake at night.

All American manned space flights are launched from Kennedy Space Center. You can see how astronauts are trained, sit in a lunar rover and try on a spacesuit.

Giant turtles lay their eggs in the sand at Melbourne. Some turtles weigh up to 800 pounds, about the same as 4 men.

Everglades Park is a huge area of grassland and swamp, where alligators live. Tropical plants with twisted roots, called mangroves, grow in the swamp.

Miami is a major tourist resort. "Coconut-watchers" make sure coconuts do not fall on the tourists' heads.

Key lime pie is a tangy dessert made with tiny yellow limes from the island of Key West.

On Key West, you can see gold from sunken ships at Mel Fisher's Treasure Exhibition.

Seminole Indians

An Indian tribe called the Seminoles live in the Everglades. They live in open-sided thatched huts, called chickees.

St.Augustine

Daytona

Cape Canaveral

Orlando

Melbourne

Tarpon Springs

Tampa

Fort Myers

Sanibel Island

Miami

Key West

Florida Keys

More Southern states

All over the Southern states there were once big farms called plantations where cotton and other crops grew. Slaves were brought from Africa to work on them. There are no longer any slaves, but many people are still poor.

◄ This map shows how the Southern states fit together.

ARKANSAS TENNESSEE MISSISSIPPI ALABAMA LOUISIANA

This gigantic statue is in the Ozark Mountains. It is called Christ of the Ozarks. It is as high as a seven-story building.

At the Ozark Folk Center, you can listen to the music and see the crafts of people who live in the Ozark Mountains.

ARKANSAS

Little Rock

Crater of Diamonds Park is the only place in the USA where diamonds are found. For a fee you can dig for them. You may keep any you are lucky enough to find.

Coca-Cola was invented in Atlanta, Georgia. You can see where it was first bottled nearly 100 years ago, at the Biedenharn Candy Museum in Vicksburg, Mississippi.

Robert de Salle was a French explorer. He travelled down the Mississippi River and claimed the land in the south for France.

Near Natchez, there is an octagonal (eight-sided) house. It is called Longwood.

Natchez

NEW ORLEANS

Marching bands play jazz music in the streets. Jazz started in New Orleans nearly 100 years ago.

Mardi Gras is the festival of Shrove Tuesday (Pancake Day). People dress up in costumes and masks. They parade the streets on decorated floats.

Part of New Orleans is known as the French Quarter. Houses here have wrought iron balconies, like those in France.

A tram ride is fun. At the end of the line, the tram seats flip over so you face the front on the way back.

Steamboats take people on cruises up the Mississippi River.

Baton Rouge

LOUISIANA

New Orleans

You can take a boat trip around a swampy area called the bayou. Alligators live there.

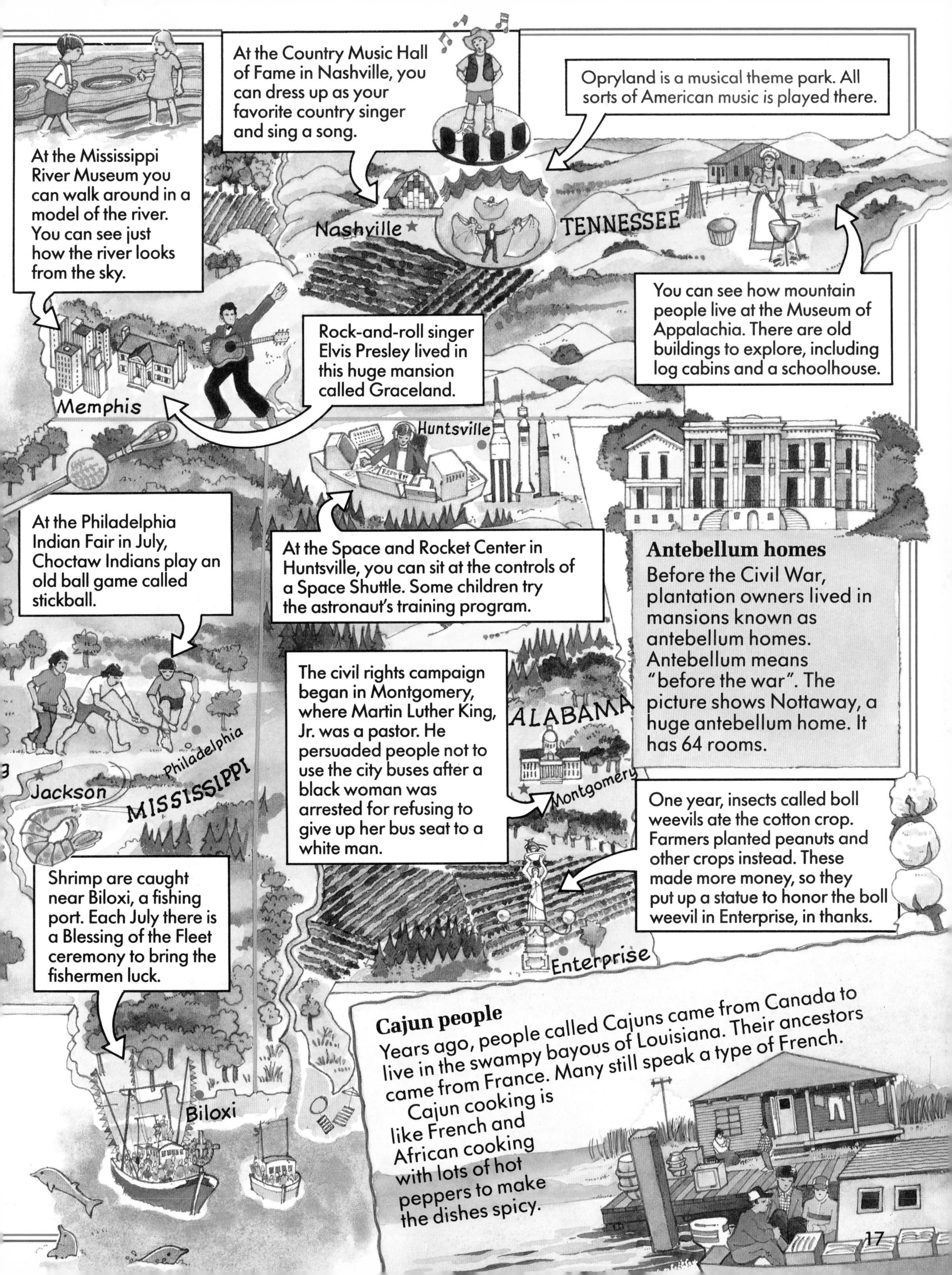

At the Country Music Hall of Fame in Nashville, you can dress up as your favorite country singer and sing a song.

Opryland is a musical theme park. All sorts of American music is played there.

At the Mississippi River Museum you can walk around in a model of the river. You can see just how the river looks from the sky.

Nashville ★

TENNESSEE

You can see how mountain people live at the Museum of Appalachia. There are old buildings to explore, including log cabins and a schoolhouse.

Rock-and-roll singer Elvis Presley lived in this huge mansion called Graceland.

Memphis

Huntsville

At the Philadelphia Indian Fair in July, Choctaw Indians play an old ball game called stickball.

At the Space and Rocket Center in Huntsville, you can sit at the controls of a Space Shuttle. Some children try the astronaut's training program.

Antebellum homes
Before the Civil War, plantation owners lived in mansions known as antebellum homes. Antebellum means "before the war". The picture shows Nottaway, a huge antebellum home. It has 64 rooms.

The civil rights campaign began in Montgomery, where Martin Luther King, Jr. was a pastor. He persuaded people not to use the city buses after a black woman was arrested for refusing to give up her bus seat to a white man.

ALABAMA

Montgomery

Philadelphia

Jackson

MISSISSIPPI

One year, insects called boll weevils ate the cotton crop. Farmers planted peanuts and other crops instead. These made more money, so they put up a statue to honor the boll weevil in Enterprise, in thanks.

Shrimp are caught near Biloxi, a fishing port. Each July there is a Blessing of the Fleet ceremony to bring the fishermen luck.

Enterprise

Cajun people
Years ago, people called Cajuns came from Canada to live in the swampy bayous of Louisiana. Their ancestors came from France. Many still speak a type of French.
Cajun cooking is like French and African cooking with lots of hot peppers to make the dishes spicy.

Biloxi

The Great Lakes

Part of each of these states borders one of the five Great Lakes. They are among the world's largest lakes. There are many smaller lakes and rivers all over this area. Boating and water sports are popular and many people own boats.

In the north, the water freezes in winter. Races are held on the ice and in some places people drive on it, too.

People tell stories of an imaginary giant lumberjack, named Paul Bunyan. They say he wrote with a pine tree pencil. At Bemidji, there are statues of Paul Bunyan and his blue ox, Babe.

Bemidji

MINNESOTA

In Itasca Park, you can cross the source of the Mississippi River on 15 stepping-stones. It flows almost 2,300m to New Orleans, in the Gulf of Mexico.

At the St. Paul winter carnival, there are ice-carving contests.

Pipestone Monument is a stone quarry. Indians use the stone to make peace pipes. You can watch the pipes being made.

St. Paul

Minneapolis

In winter, it is sometimes so cold that schools are closed. in Minneapolis, there are enclosed skywalks between many buildings so people can get around without going outside.

The House on the Rock at Spring Green is built into natural curves in the rock. One room juts out. It has thousands of windows, including one in the floor with a view of the valley far below.

CHICAGO

The vast city of Chicago is the "crossroads" of the USA. It has a huge port, as well as the world's largest railway yards and busiest airport. It is an important center for industry, banking, and grain and cattle markets.

"Deep dish" pizza was first made in Chicago. It has a thick crust and is covered in cheese.

There are cheese factories all over Wisconsin. Some of them give tours so you can see how cheese is made.

Long ago, cattle roamed free on the plains. Then an Illinois farmer invented barbed wire. Cattle could now be kept in one area.

The Sears Tower is the world's tallest building. It is 1,462ft high. You can take an elevator to the top. On a clear day, you can see four states: Illinois, Indiana, Michigan and Wisconsin.

There is lots to see at the Museum of Science and Industry, including a model of a working coal mine.

Some trains run on tracks above street level. They are known as "els", short for elevated railways.

President Abraham Lincoln was once a lawyer in Springfield. During the Civil War, he freed the slaves and helped the Union to win.

There are so many lakes in Minnesota that it is known as the Land of 10,000 Lakes. In fact, there are even more than this number.

Mackinac Bridge is almost 5m long. It connects the two parts of Michigan.

Indians of the Eastern Woodlands

Indian tribes once lived in the woods by the lakes and rivers. They went hunting and trading in canoes made out of birch bark. Some tribes also made birch bark homes, called wigwams.

Cars are not allowed on Mackinac Island. Visitors must travel by carriage, horse, bicycle or on foot.

Many German people settled in Milwaukee. They were skilled at brewing and the town has become well-known for its beer.

Many Dutch people settled in the town of Holland. A huge 200 year old windmill is one of many Dutch things to see here.

Detroit is known as Motor City because so many cars are made there. The first car built in Detroit was made by Henry Ford in 1896. His Model T Ford cars were cheap and very popular.

Indianapolis is famous for car racing. At the Indy 500 festival each year, cars compete at speeds of over 180m per hour.

There are antique popcorn machines on show at the Wyandotte Popcorn Museum in Marion. There's plenty of popcorn to try, too.

The largest children's museum in the world is in Indianapolis. Exhibits include an old-fashioned carousel and lots of toy trains.

At King's Island amusement park in Mason, there is the world's longest roller coaster, called The Beast.

Map labels: WISCONSIN, MICHIGAN, Mackinac Island, Holland, Lansing, Milwaukee, Detroit, Cleveland, Marion, Chicago, INDIANA, OHIO, Columbus, ILLINOIS, Springfield, Indianapolis, Mason, Cincinatti

The Great Plains

Across the middle of the USA lies the prairie – a vast, flat, dry and windy area known as the Great Plains. Few trees grow. It is mostly wheat fields and grassland, where cattle graze. Great herds of buffalo once roamed the Plains. They were nearly all killed by settlers, who hunted them for sport.

▼ This map shows how the states of the Great Plains fit together.

NORTH DAKOTA
SOUTH DAKOTA
IOWA
NEBRASKA
MISSOURI
KANSAS
OKLAHOMA

North Dakota is the coldest state in the United States, after Alaska.

This colossal mountain carving is at Mount Rushmore. It shows the heads of four Presidents: George Washington, Thomas Jefferson, Abraham Lincoln and Theodore Roosevelt.

Indians of the Plains

Many Indian tribes, such as the Blackfeet and Apache, lived on the Plains. They hunted the buffalo and killed enough to eat. They used the skins for tents and clothes.

Years ago, farmers ploughed up the grass to raise crops on the Plains. The soil became dry and blew away. Nothing would grow. The area became known as the Dust Bowl. In the end, people learned better ways of farming and crops grew again. Today most of the USA's wheat and corn is grown here.

A pile of stones marks the center of the North American continent at Rugby.

The World's Largest Buffalo is an enormous statue near Jamestown. It is in memory of the buffaloes that lived on the prairie.

The Corn Palace in Mitchell is decorated all over with corn and other grains. Every autumn fresh grain is added for birds and squirrels to eat during winter.

Rugby

NORTH DAKOTA

Bismarck

Jamestown

SOUTH DAKOTA

Pierre

Mitchell

In Badlands Park, the colorful rocks are twisted into weird spirals and ridges.

This mountain carving is of Crazy Horse, a Sioux Indian chief. It is not yet finished. There is a model nearby to show you what it will look like. At almost 650ft, it will be the world's tallest statue.

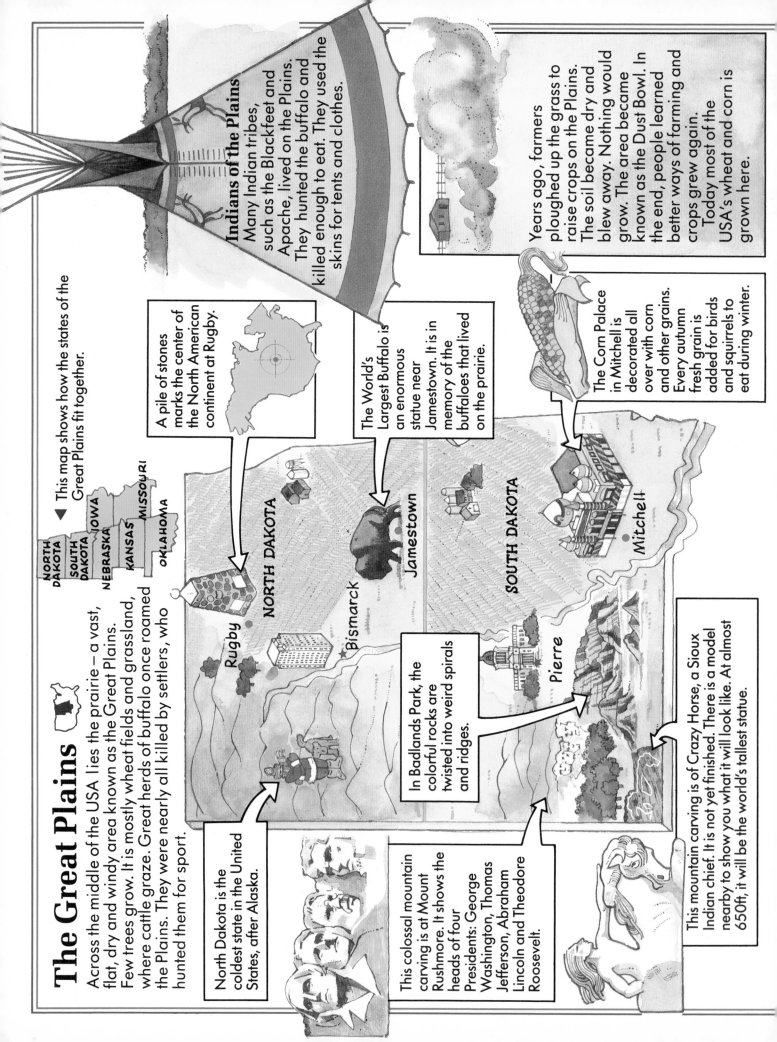

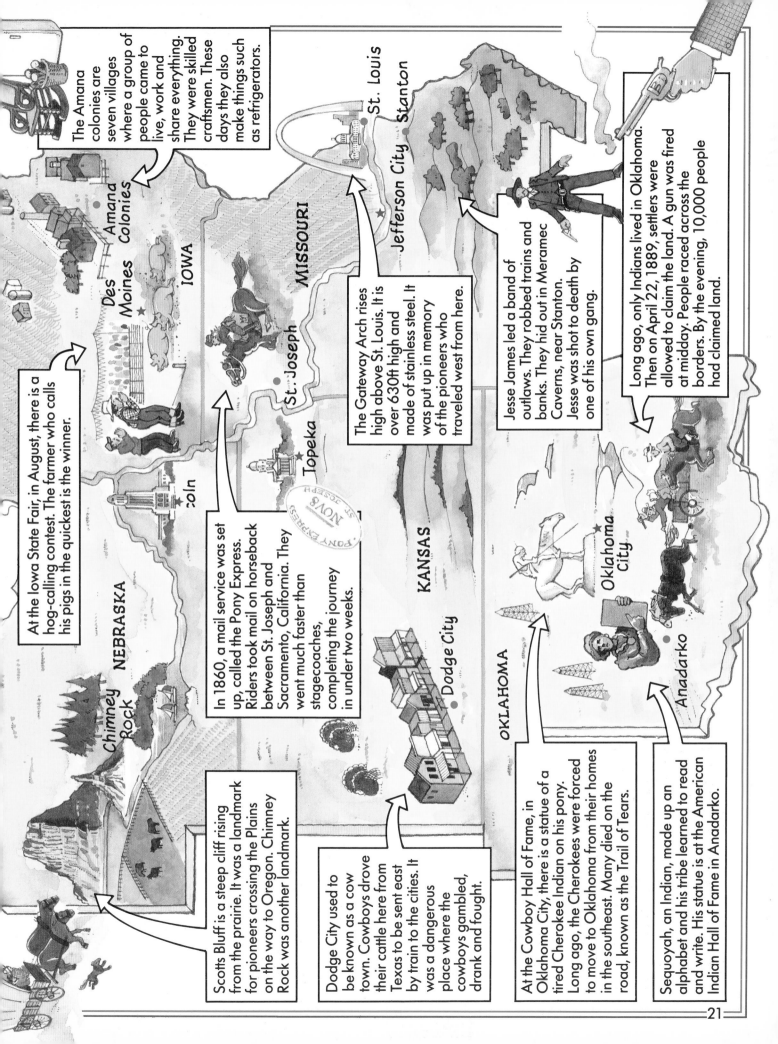

The Amana colonies are seven villages where a group of people came to live, work and share everything. They were skilled craftsmen. These days they also make things such as refrigerators.

The Gateway Arch rises high above St. Louis. It is over 630ft high and made of stainless steel. It was put up in memory of the pioneers who traveled west from here.

Jesse James led a band of outlaws. They robbed trains and banks. They hid out in Meramec Caverns, near Stanton. Jesse was shot to death by one of his own gang.

Long ago, only Indians lived in Oklahoma. Then on April 22, 1889, settlers were allowed to claim the land. A gun was fired at midday. People raced across the borders. By the evening, 10,000 people had claimed land.

St. Louis • Stanton

Jefferson City

MISSOURI

St. Joseph

IOWA

Des Moines

Amana Colonies

NEBRASKA

At the Iowa State Fair, in August, there is a hog-calling contest. The farmer who calls his pigs in the quickest is the winner.

In 1860, a mail service was set up, called the Pony Express. Riders took mail on horseback between St. Joseph and Sacramento, California. They went much faster than stagecoaches, completing the journey in under two weeks.

PONY EXPRESS NOV 8 ST. JOSEPH

Topeka

KANSAS

coln

Chimney Rock

Scotts Bluff is a steep cliff rising from the prairie. It was a landmark for pioneers crossing the Plains on the way to Oregon. Chimney Rock was another landmark.

Dodge City used to be known as a cow town. Cowboys drove their cattle here from Texas to be sent east by train to the cities. It was a dangerous place where the cowboys gambled, drank and fought.

• Dodge City

OKLAHOMA

Oklahoma City

Anadarko

At the Cowboy Hall of Fame, in Oklahoma City, there is a statue of a tired Cherokee Indian on his pony. Long ago, the Cherokees were forced to move to Oklahoma from their homes in the southeast. Many died on the road, known as the Trail of Tears.

Sequoyah, an Indian, made up an alphabet and his tribe learned to read and write. His statue is at the American Indian Hall of Fame in Anadarko.

21

Texas

Texas is the second largest state after Alaska. People say that most things in Texas are big. Even the beef steaks are huge. Texas is so big it can snow in the north of the state while it is scorching hot in the south. Sometimes there are violent whirlwinds called tornadoes.

Texas was once part of Mexico. Lots of Mexicans live in Texas today. Texans like eating a spicy mixture of Texan and Mexican food, known as Tex-Mex.

The Indians dug colored flint from a quarry near Alibates. They made it into tools and weapons.

This part of Texas is known as a "panhandle", a strip of land sticking out into another state. Alaska, Idaho, Oklahoma and Florida also have panhandles.

The world's largest cattle auction is held in Amarillo.

A Cowboy Morning is fun to take part in. You travel by horse-drawn wagon to the rim of Palo Duro Canyon. Then you dig into a hearty cowboy breakfast round the campfire.

Windmills are used in dry areas to pump water from deep underground. Sometimes they are the colors of the Texan flag.

At Indian Cliff Dude Ranch in El Paso, you can join a trail ride into the desert.

Fort Davis was built to protect travellers on the road west from being attacked by Indians. It has been restored so you can see how the soldiers lived.

The Paseo del Rio in San Antonio is a path which follows the San Antonio River through the middle of the town. It looks pretty when it is lit with colored lights at night.

People take rough, exciting boat trips down a river called the Rio Grande. It winds through deep canyons in Big Bend Park.

Sea World

There are all sorts of sea creatures at Sea World in San Antonio, including penguins and dolphins. One show features killer whales, who make spectacular leaps from the water.

People enjoy water sports all over Texas. Tubing (floating in inner tubes) down the Guadalupe River is very popular.

Lots of spinach grows near Crystal City. There is a statue in the town of the cartoon character Popeye; the Sailor Man. He loves eating spinach to make him strong.

Amarillo

El Paso

Fort Davis

Crystal City

There are lots of dinosaur skeletons at the Fort Worth Museum of Science and History. These two look as though they are locked in combat.

Six Flags Over Texas was the first in a chain of amusement parks. It is called Six Flags because Texas has been ruled by six different governments in its history.

The Dallas Cowboys are a very successful American football team. They also have a well-known team of cheerleaders (girls who lead the crowd in cheering).

This area was once the world's largest oilfield. Oil brought wealth to towns, known as "boom towns". You can walk around a copy of an old boom town at the museum in Kilgore.

Oil is pumped all over Texas. These sorts of pumps are nicknamed "nodding donkeys" because that is what they look like.

Dallas

Fort Worth

Kilgore

Mission Control for space flights to the moon is at the Lyndon B. Johnson Space Center in Houston. Things to see there include Apollo spacecraft and lunar rocks.

Ranches
There are vast cattle ranches in Texas. Longhorn cattle are kept on some ranches. They have very long, curved horns and red and white hides.

Austin

Houston

The Alamo is an old building in San Antonio. In 1836, at the siege of the Alamo, Davy Crockett and a band of men fought off the Mexican army. The Texans lost and many were killed.

The Astrodome in Houston was the first air-conditioned indoor stadium in the world. Baseball and American football are played there.

Spanish missions
All over Texas the Spanish built places called missions where they taught the Indians about Christianity and the Spanish way of life. The picture shows Mission San José in San Antonio.

In the village of Los Ebanos, a hand-pulled ferry crosses the Rio Grande to Mexico and back. Stagecoaches and wagons used to cross the same way.

banos

The Desert

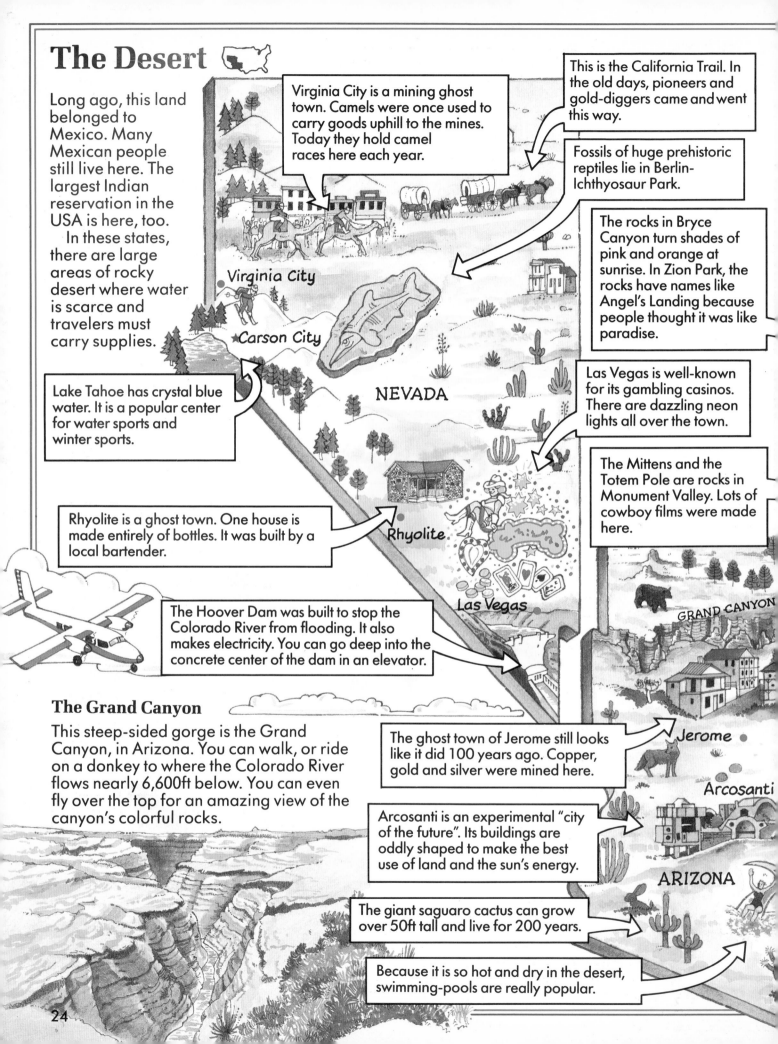

Long ago, this land belonged to Mexico. Many Mexican people still live here. The largest Indian reservation in the USA is here, too.

In these states, there are large areas of rocky desert where water is scarce and travelers must carry supplies.

Virginia City is a mining ghost town. Camels were once used to carry goods uphill to the mines. Today they hold camel races here each year.

This is the California Trail. In the old days, pioneers and gold-diggers came and went this way.

Fossils of huge prehistoric reptiles lie in Berlin-Ichthyosaur Park.

The rocks in Bryce Canyon turn shades of pink and orange at sunrise. In Zion Park, the rocks have names like Angel's Landing because people thought it was like paradise.

Lake Tahoe has crystal blue water. It is a popular center for water sports and winter sports.

Las Vegas is well-known for its gambling casinos. There are dazzling neon lights all over the town.

Rhyolite is a ghost town. One house is made entirely of bottles. It was built by a local bartender.

The Mittens and the Totem Pole are rocks in Monument Valley. Lots of cowboy films were made here.

The Hoover Dam was built to stop the Colorado River from flooding. It also makes electricity. You can go deep into the concrete center of the dam in an elevator.

The Grand Canyon

This steep-sided gorge is the Grand Canyon, in Arizona. You can walk, or ride on a donkey to where the Colorado River flows nearly 6,600ft below. You can even fly over the top for an amazing view of the canyon's colorful rocks.

The ghost town of Jerome still looks like it did 100 years ago. Copper, gold and silver were mined here.

Arcosanti is an experimental "city of the future". Its buildings are oddly shaped to make the best use of land and the sun's energy.

The giant saguaro cactus can grow over 50ft tall and live for 200 years.

Because it is so hot and dry in the desert, swimming-pools are really popular.

Virginia City
Carson City
NEVADA
Rhyolite
Las Vegas
GRAND CANYON
Jerome
Arcosanti
ARIZONA

The Great Salt Lake is very salty. It is almost impossible for a bather to sink because salt helps you float.

This map shows how these four states fit together.

NEVADA UTAH COLORADO
ARIZONA NEW MEXICO

Salt Lake City

A religious group called the Mormons set up the state of Utah. They built this huge temple in Salt Lake City.

Four Corners is the only place in the USA where you can be in four states at once. Utah, Colorado, New Mexico and Arizona meet here.

UTAH

In Arches Park, the wind and water have worn away the stone into strange shapes, including more than 200 arches.

Pueblos

Some Indians built towns of adobe (mud bricks). These towns are called pueblos. Many pueblos are in New Mexico. Taos is the largest one.

Rainbow Bridge is the world's largest natural bridge.

At Red Rock the Zuni Indian tribe holds a colorful ceremony. Dancers dress as bird-like spirits called kachinas.

Billy the Kid committed more than 20 murders. He was shot by the sheriff, Pat Garrett, and buried at Fort Sumner.

NEW MEXICO

Taos

Meteor Crater was formed when a vast meteorite crashed to earth thousands of years ago.

Santa Fe

Red Rock

Fort Sumner

In Petrified Forest Park, there are colorful fossils of tree trunks. They are millions of years old, but they look alive.

Albuquerque

People come to Albuquerque for hot-air ballooning because it usually has dry weather and a cloudless sky.

Old Tucson was built as a film set. It looks like Tucson town did in the 1860s. Today there are stagecoach rides and mock gunfights.

There are huge underground caves at Carlsbad. Every evening thousands of bats leave the caves in search of insects.

Mountain lions and bighorn sheep are desert animals. You can see them at the Arizona-Sonora Desert Museum.

At White Sands Monument there are brilliant white sand dunes made of a mineral called gypsum.

Carlsbad

The Rocky Mountains

The Rocky Mountain range is the longest in North America. It crosses several states including Montana, Wyoming and Colorado. People come here for sports such as skiing, fishing and riding and to enjoy the beautiful scenery. You may see bears, moose and other wild animals.

From Going-to-the-Sun Road in Glacier Park, there are fine views of mountain lakes and glaciers. You might see a bald eagle, the American national bird.

Clark carved his name on this rock. It is called Pompey's Pillar after Little Pomp, Sacagawea's son.

After they had attacked an Indian camp, General Custer and all his army were killed by Sioux and Cheyenne warriors at the Battle of the Little Bighorn in 1876.

A powwow is an Indian festival. You can sleep in a teepee at the Crow Fair powwow in August.

Devil's Tower is a huge volcanic rock. It rises sharply out of the flat prairie. You can see it from far away.

A rodeo is a display of cowboys' skills. The Wild Horse Stampede is a very tough rodeo. It is held at Wolf Point in July.

Long ago, steamboats puffed up the Missouri River to transport goods to and from St. Louis.

Buffalo Bill was a buffalo hunter and showman. His Wild West Show was popular all over the country and in Europe. You can learn about him at the museum in Cody.

In areas without roads, firefighters parachute in to attack forest fires. This is called smokejumping. You can see how it is done at Missoula's Aerial Fire Depot.

Madison Buffalo Jump is a steep cliff. Plains Indians used to kill buffalo by herding them into a stampede over the cliff.

Virginia City and Nevada City are restored ghost towns. People once came to pan for gold. Today, you can walk the wooden sidewalks and peer into saloons and stores.

Wolf Point

MONTANA

Cody

Helena

Missoula

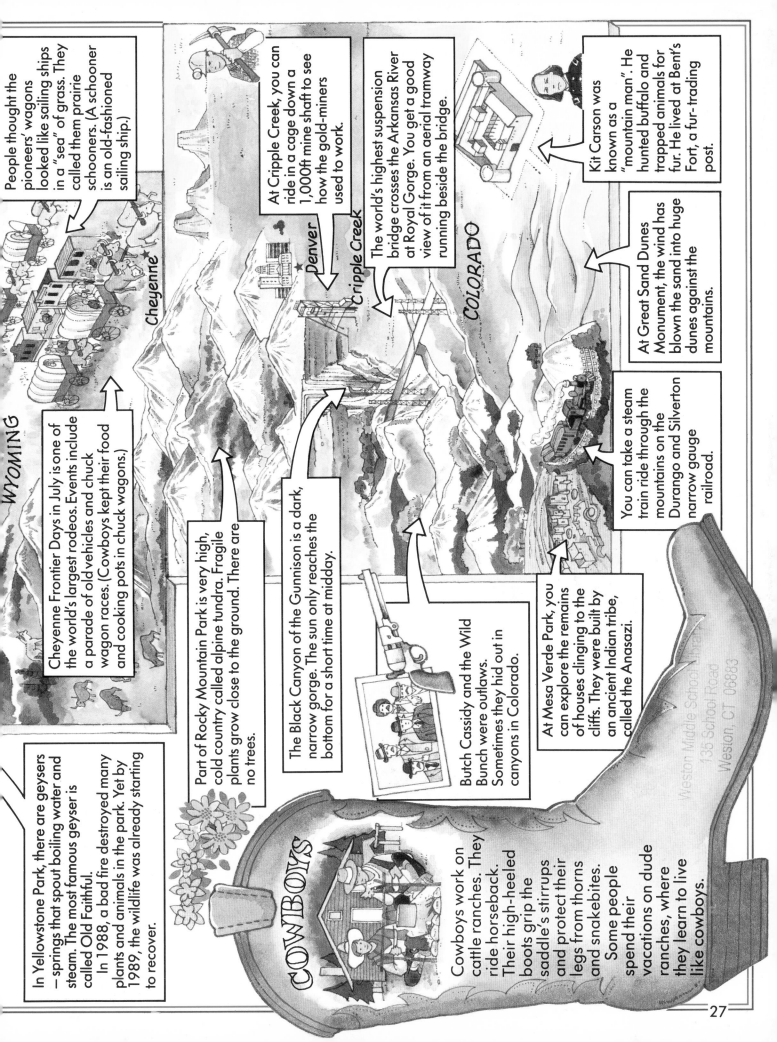

People thought the pioneers' wagons looked like sailing ships in a "sea" of grass. They called them prairie schooners. (A schooner is an old-fashioned sailing ship.)

Cheyenne

WYOMING

Cheyenne Frontier Days in July is one of the world's largest rodeos. Events include a parade of old vehicles and chuck wagon races. (Cowboys kept their food and cooking pots in chuck wagons.)

At Cripple Creek, you can ride in a cage down a 1,000ft mine shaft to see how the gold-miners used to work.

Denver

Cripple Creek

The world's highest suspension bridge crosses the Arkansas River at Royal Gorge. You get a good view of it from an aerial tramway running beside the bridge.

Kit Carson was known as a "mountain man". He hunted buffalo and trapped animals for fur. He lived at Bent's Fort, a fur-trading post.

COLORADO

At Great Sand Dunes Monument, the wind has blown the sand into huge dunes against the mountains.

In Yellowstone Park, there are geysers – springs that spout boiling water and steam. The most famous geyser is called Old Faithful.
In 1988, a bad fire destroyed many plants and animals in the park. Yet by 1989, the wildlife was already starting to recover.

Part of Rocky Mountain Park is very high, cold country called alpine tundra. Fragile plants grow close to the ground. There are no trees.

The Black Canyon of the Gunnison is a dark, narrow gorge. The sun only reaches the bottom for a short time at midday.

Butch Cassidy and the Wild Bunch were outlaws. Sometimes they hid out in canyons in Colorado.

At Mesa Verde Park, you can explore the remains of houses clinging to the cliffs. They were built by an ancient Indian tribe, called the Anasazi.

You can take a steam train ride through the mountains on the Durango and Silverton narrow gauge railroad.

COWBOYS

Cowboys work on cattle ranches. They ride horseback. Their high-heeled boots grip the saddle's stirrups and protect their legs from thorns and snakebites.
Some people spend their vacations on dude ranches, where they learn to live like cowboys.

Alaska and the Northwest

Alaska is the largest state in the USA, but the fewest people live there. Northern Alaska is the bleak and snowy Arctic region. Further south, there are icy mountains and pine forests.

In the northwest states, it is often very rainy, especially near the coast. There are lots of volcanoes, craters and lava flows to see.

This map shows ▶ Alaska and the northwest states. Alaska is very far away, separated from the rest of the USA by Canada.

Alaska
CANADA
Idaho
Washington
Oregon

Prudhoe Bay is the largest oil field in North America. The oil is piped across Alaska through the Trans-Alaska Pipeline.

The Arctic Circle is an imaginary circle, round the top of the earth. North of the line, the sun does not set in midsummer, or rise in midwinter.

It is too cold for trees to grow north of here. Where they stop growing is called the tree line.

Nome

Each year there is a dogsled race all the way from Anchorage to Nome.

This town is called North Pole. Some children send letters here addressed to Santa Claus.

North Pole

ALASKA

Mount McKinley is the highest mountain in North America. It is 20,320ft high.

Anchorage

On Good Friday in 1964, Anchorage was hit by the strongest earthquake ever recorded in North America. Today it is a popular winter sports resort.

In 1989, an oil tanker ran aground in Prince William Bay. Oil spread along the coast killing many plants and animals.

Eskimos

There are several groups of native Alaskans. One group is the Eskimos. Some Eskimos made their homes, called igloos, from blocks of ice. These days Eskimos mostly live in houses.

Tossing someone in a blanket is an Eskimo game. It is played at festivals.

Kodiak Island

Brown bears live on Kodiak Island. They are very fond of salmon, which they fish out of streams with their paws.

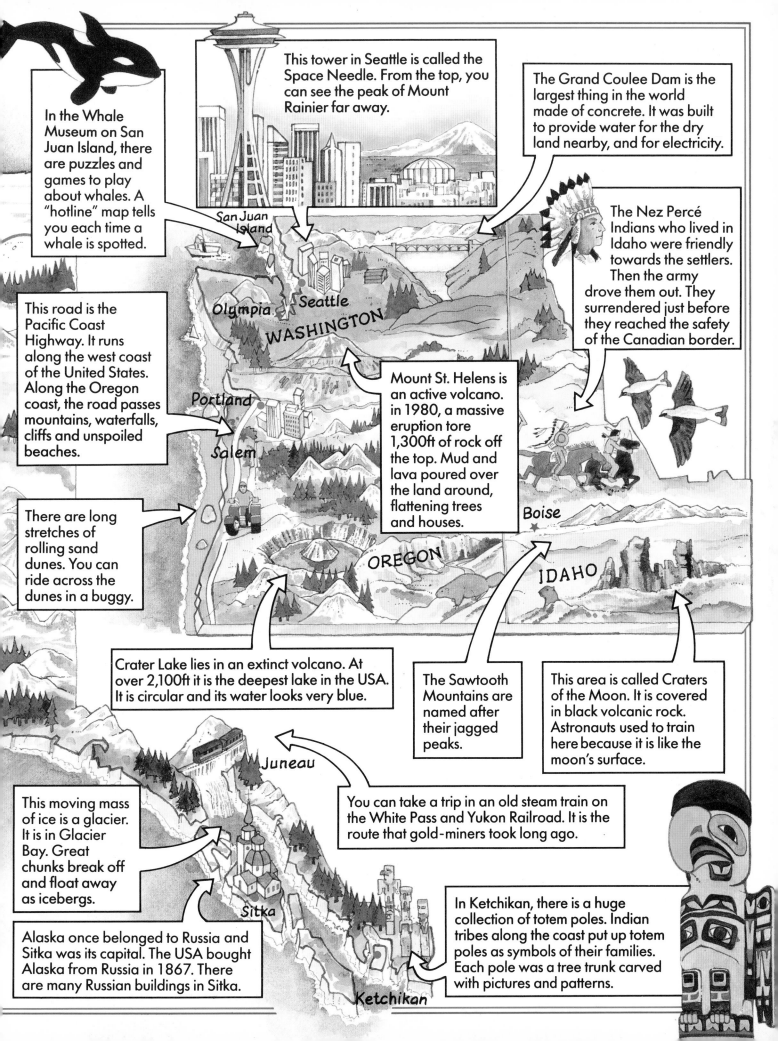

In the Whale Museum on San Juan Island, there are puzzles and games to play about whales. A "hotline" map tells you each time a whale is spotted.

This tower in Seattle is called the Space Needle. From the top, you can see the peak of Mount Rainier far away.

The Grand Coulee Dam is the largest thing in the world made of concrete. It was built to provide water for the dry land nearby, and for electricity.

The Nez Percé Indians who lived in Idaho were friendly towards the settlers. Then the army drove them out. They surrendered just before they reached the safety of the Canadian border.

This road is the Pacific Coast Highway. It runs along the west coast of the United States. Along the Oregon coast, the road passes mountains, waterfalls, cliffs and unspoiled beaches.

Mount St. Helens is an active volcano. in 1980, a massive eruption tore 1,300ft of rock off the top. Mud and lava poured over the land around, flattening trees and houses.

There are long stretches of rolling sand dunes. You can ride across the dunes in a buggy.

Crater Lake lies in an extinct volcano. At over 2,100ft it is the deepest lake in the USA. It is circular and its water looks very blue.

The Sawtooth Mountains are named after their jagged peaks.

This area is called Craters of the Moon. It is covered in black volcanic rock. Astronauts used to train here because it is like the moon's surface.

This moving mass of ice is a glacier. It is in Glacier Bay. Great chunks break off and float away as icebergs.

You can take a trip in an old steam train on the White Pass and Yukon Railroad. It is the route that gold-miners took long ago.

Alaska once belonged to Russia and Sitka was its capital. The USA bought Alaska from Russia in 1867. There are many Russian buildings in Sitka.

In Ketchikan, there is a huge collection of totem poles. Indian tribes along the coast put up totem poles as symbols of their families. Each pole was a tree trunk carved with pictures and patterns.

San Juan Island

Olympia

Seattle

WASHINGTON

Portland

Salem

Boise

OREGON

IDAHO

Juneau

Sitka

Ketchikan

California

There are several different climates in California. In the north, it is mild and wet, while in the south, it is hot. In the eastern part of the state, there are mountains and desert. In many parts of

California, earthquakes may happen, so most houses are single-storyed. They are mainly built of wood, which bends, as brick houses would crack and collapse when the ground shakes.

At the Wells Fargo Bank museum, you can send a coded message by telegraph and sit in a model of an old stagecoach.

SAN FRANCISCO

Actually, the famous Golden Gate bridge is red. On most mornings, clouds of fog roll under it.

A special bread called sourdough is made in San Francisco. Fermented dough is used to make the bread rise. It tastes quite salty.

Giant sequoias are the world's most massive trees. They grow in mountain areas. The largest of all is in Sequoia Park. It is called General Sherman and it is over 102ft around the trunk.

The best way to get up and down the steep streets is to take a bumpy ride in a cable car. They are drawn along by thick, strong wire under the street.

You can test your senses at the Exploratorium. For instance, find out why standing in this special room can make you feel like a giant.

Lava Beds Monument is an area of black lava rock. There are hundreds of caves to explore.

In 1848, gold was found at Sutter's Mill. In 1849, a "gold rush" started. People from many countries came seeking gold. They were known as "forty-niners".

Yosemite Park is a beautiful mountain area. It is popular for hiking.

Coastal redwoods are the tallest trees in the world. They grow in Redwood Park and along the northern California coast, where the weather is foggy.

Grapes are grown in the Napa Valley. They are made into wine.

Sacramento

San Francisco

The lowest point in North America is in Death Valley. It is very hot and dry. You must take plenty of water if you visit the area.

Strange plants, called Joshuas, can be seen growing in the desert at Joshua Tree Monument. The area is carpeted with flowers in spring.

Long ago, the Spanish set up 21 religious missions along the California coast. Mission San Juan Capistrano is famous for the swallows that return every year on March 19, St Joseph's Day.

California grows more fruit and vegetables than any other state. Crops include almonds and apricots.

A farmer named Walter Knott crossed blackberries and raspberries to make boysenberries. His farm, Knott's Berry Farm, is now an amusement park.

San Diego Zoo has a huge number of animals. Take the aerial tramway or the double-decker bus for the best views of the zoo.

Anaheim

Los Angeles

San Diego

Disneyland

Disneyland, in Anaheim, was the world's first theme park. It was set up by Walt Disney, who created Mickey Mouse and other animated characters. There are lots of exciting and scary rides. Some are based on well-known stories, such as Sleeping Beauty.

© The Walt Disney Company

Along the coast of southern California, there are wide, sandy beaches. People enjoy surfing the great waves that roll in from the Pacific Ocean.

The tram tour of Universal Studios takes you around several film sets. The ride also takes you through adventures such as a tunnel of ice and a collapsing bridge.

LOS ANGELES

In winter, people go on boat trips to watch Pacific grey whales.

There are many freeways (expressways). A number of them cross over at this point, known as "the stack".

Long ago, mammoths and other animals were trapped in bubbling tar pits at La Brea. Their bones are in the museum there.

Index

First published 1990 by Usborne Publishing Ltd, Usborne House, 83-85 Saffron Hill, London EC1N 8RT

Copyright © Usborne Publishing Ltd, 1990.
The name Usborne and the device ⊛ are Trade Marks of Usborne Publishing Ltd.

Printed in Belgium.   American edition 1990.